This book belongs to:

Quarto is the authority on a wide range of topics.

Quarto educates, entertains and enriches the lives of our readers—enthusiasts and lovers of hands-on living.

www.quartoknows.com

Author and Illustrator: Steve Smallman
Designer: Victoria Kimonidou
Editor: Harriet Stone

This edition first published in 2018 by QED Publishing,
an imprint of The Quarto Group.
The Old Brewery, 6 Blundell Street,
London N7 9BH, United Kingdom.
T (0)20 7700 6700 F (0)20 7700 8066
www.QuartoKnows.com

A catalogue record for this book is available from the British Library.

ISBN 978 1 91241 389 8

Manufactured in Guangdong, China CC072018

9 8 7 6 5 4 3 2 1

MIX
Paper from
responsible sources
FSC® C008047
www.fsc.org

by STEVE SMALLMAN

THE NOT-SO-BRAVE PENGUIN

Percy penguin wasn't scared of anything.
He loved **WHIZZING** down
snowy slopes on his tummy.

Posy penguin was not so brave.
She shuffled down slopes
on her bottom instead.

Posy didn't jump,
she was scared
she might do
a belly flop.

SPLASH!

Percy loved jumping into the water with a great big

Posy was scared of lots of things...

...snowstorms,

...heights,

...loud noises.

But most of all she was scared of...

BOo!

...THE DARK!

When the penguins huddled together
at night she would stare out at the
BIG BLACK EMPTINESS
around her and imagine
all the scary things that
might be out there.

One morning the penguins woke to find a **HUGE** iceberg floating close to their island.

Percy thought it looked amazing!
Posy thought it looked scary.

Percy leapt into the sea
and swam over to explore.

The iceberg was like a
PENGUIN PLAYGROUND!
There were slides EVERYWHERE!

Percy played for ages.
He was having a fantastic
time until he whizzed down
an ice slide too fast.

He CRASHED into a dark
cave and bumped his head.

"Percy hasn't come back!" cried Posy,
standing on the shore that evening.

"You worry too much,"
said the other penguins.
"Percy will be fine."

But Posy was sure that something was wrong.
Then she did a very brave thing...

she **JUMPED** into the
sea and swam over to
the huge iceberg.

"Percy, where are you?"
she cried, looking around.
There was no answer.

Then Posy saw footprints.
She followed them up to the
top of a big slippery slide.

"He must have gone down there!" she gulped.

Posy took a deep breath and slid down the slide,

FASTER

and FASTER,

straight into a
SCARY CAVE!

"OOF!"

Posy's feet hit something soft. It was Percy!
He had a big bump on his head.

"Posy?" he asked groggily. "How did you get here?"

"I jumped and swam and climbed and slid, until I bumped into your bottom," said Posy.

"WOW!" said Percy. "That was brave. Weren't you scared?"

"Yes. And I still am because now it's... DARK!"

"But it isn't really dark," said Percy. "Look!"

The sky wasn't black and empty. It was BEAUTIFUL.
All green and blue. Posy didn't feel so scared anymore.

Posy and Percy snuggled up
to keep warm, and after a
while they fell fast asleep.

The next morning Percy's head was feeling much better and they were ready to swim back home.

"Thank you for rescuing me, Posy," said Percy. "That was very brave of you!"

"Ooh!" said Posy with a grin,
"I never knew I was brave!"

Percy smiled. "Well, you helped me even
though you were scared, which makes you the

BRAVEST PENGUIN OF ALL!"

NEXT STEPS

Discussion and comprehension

Discuss the story with the children and ask the following questions, encouraging them to take turns and give full answers if they are able to. Offer support by turning to the appropriate pages of the book if needed.

- Where do you think this story is set?
- Why was Posy scared to jump into the water?
- What is Posy scared of the most? Why?
- At the end of the story Percy told Posy that she was the bravest penguin of all. Why did he say that?

Being scared and being brave

Discuss what an amazing character Posy is for overcoming her fears and being brave when it was needed most. Ask the children to think of things that they are scared of. Write two headings on a piece of paper: 'I am scared of...' and 'I could be brave by...' Tell the children what you are most scared of and write it under the first heading. Then tell them how you could be brave like Posy, and write it under the second heading. E.g. 'I am scared of spiders.' 'I could be brave by holding a spider in my hand for one minute.' Give the children a piece of paper with the two headings at the top. Ask them to write their responses under each heading. When they have finished, ask them to read out their first sentence in a scared voice and their second sentence in a brave voice.

Percy and Posy pictures

Start by having a look at the illustration of the penguins and the iceberg on page 12. Give each child a piece of blue sugar paper and some white paint. Begin the activity by asking the children to paint the iceberg from the book and finger paint some snowflakes in the sky. Give each child two black sugar paper ovals for the penguins' bodies, four googly eyes and two orange card triangles for the beaks. Encourage the children to glue the bodies, eyes and beaks onto their snowy picture, to make Percy and Posy. Once the shapes are stuck on, the children can paint a white patch on the front of each penguin and flippers on the sides. Finally give the children a small amount of orange paint and show them how to finger paint feet at the bottom of each penguin.